GRANDMA'S PURSE
OF *love*

written by Cindy Noorda

Printed in the United States of America by Piles of Love Books
www.pilesoflovebooks.com

ISBN-13: 978-0-9966560-1-6

Library of Congress Control Number: 2015948037

The text of this book is set in 18pt Minion Pro font.
The illustrations in this book were created using watercolor and charcoal.

With love, for my Mother

Love and thanks to my family for sharing with me their advice, encouragement, and creative suggestions. My heartfelt thanks to Amariah, whose darling illustrations bring all my words to life. I could not have done this without all of you.

Within the walls of Grandma's home
You'll find her Piles of Love.
Each visible, each rooted deep-
So many cherished things to keep.

As you will discover, these small piles of clutter
Are treasures she'll never let go.
Carefully saved and stacked up quite neat
Are the things that make Grandma's home unique!

There are piles of books
To be placed in a box;
Piles of pictures
She doesn't want lost.

Piles of clothing
No one will wear;
There are piles of grandchildren,
Everywhere!

There are piles of old records
And games to be played;
Piles of creations
Her children have made.

There are piles to be written
And piles to be read
There are piles stuffed neatly
Under her bed.

There are piles in the kitchen
Just waiting to bake.
Piles of crafts
For Grandma to make!

There are piles of animals
Needing her love,
Her soft gentle lap,
Her kisses and hugs!

There are piles of old sweaters
All snuggly and warm;
Piles of her hats
That are tattered and torn.

There are piles of shoes
With both low and high heels-
There are piles, I'm sure,
No thief would dare steal!

There are piles for her quilting,
And piles for her sewing;
And piles for each holiday
Continually growing!

There are piles of collections
From buttons to bows;
Piles of silk flowers,
And baskets in droves!

There are piles of lists,
Coupons, and bills-
Lipstick and jewelry,
Perfume and pills.

There are piles labeled "dirty"
And piles labeled "clean;"
Piles to be mended,
Ironed, and steamed!

The piles just keep piling
In heaps on the floor;
There are piles in the hallway-
The closet has more!

There are "things to do" piles,
And piles that just sit.
Pillows and blankets-
Oh, piles that won't quit!

There are piles to be donated,
Piles to be kept.
Piles by the rug,
That need to be swept!

There are piles to be eaten,
And piles to be mailed-
Yes, in the fridge,
There are piles going stale!

There are piles on piles,
And piles out of place.
Piles on the counter-
Every corner and space!

There are piles on the steps,
And piles by the stairs!
Oh, please don't sit down
There's a pile on that chair!

There are piles of candy
For each Halloween;
Birthdays and Holidays
And most days between!

Oh, never touch a pile!
Because if you do
You may lose Grandma's
Best recipe for stew!

There are piles of scrapbooks
Tied up with twine.
Piles of fridge magnets
Pleading, "Don't Whine!"

Piles of catalogs
And "old" junk mail,
There are piles of ads
For anything on sale!!

There are piles to ignore
And never acknowledge.
Piles for the grads
Who are heading to college!

Piles of mints
For all of her friends;
So much kindness-
It just never ends!

Some piles move around
And you never know where;
Some are forgotten
In the basement downstairs.

Some piles tell a story
Of a trip far away
Some tell of history
Some are havens for play.

Some piles are heirlooms,
So precious and dear;
Some piles for Grandma
Bring back a few tears.

So many piles waiting…
To be cleared away.
Just waiting…says Grandma,
"For a quiet, rainy day."

But time gently passes,
And somehow we knew.
That rainy day would come
When her life here was through.

Then all her loved treasures,
The memories too;
Will be gathered together
And piled someplace new.

Somewhere in our hearts-
A sacred new place-
A trunk in the attic,
A box, or aged case.

There they will move,
All the tales of her life.
The piles upon piles
Of happiness and strife.

Her trinkets and treasures,
The heirlooms of time-
The liked and adored things,
Her laughter that binds.

In each of our homes,
We will keep her sweet things.
That filled all her hopes,
Her wishes and dreams!

Her cherished possessions
Will lay peaceful inside.
And Grandma's relief
Can be heard with a sigh.

In each of our homes,
We will keep her sweet things.
That filled all her hopes,
Her wishes and dreams!

Her cherished possessions
Will lay peaceful inside.
And Grandma's relief
Can be heard with a sigh.

She'll look down upon us
And smile from above.
Content that we've saved
All her 'Piles of Love.'

23230653R00029

Made in the USA
Middletown, DE
19 August 2015